My name is Chan ya'll today is the day that I am marring the love of my life Lamar! Today is April 24th 1993 and today is my wedding day! I woke up in a rush as I have to get my babies up and dress quickly. Mika three years old and Nicole 6 months. As I am dressing Nicole she is rubbing my belly. You guessed it I am 2 months pregnant. I had no idea that there would be some much left to do on my wedding day. Since there is still so many things that I need to personally check on I am getting the kids ready ready to go to their grandmothers. While getting them dressed I am going over my check list in my head. I am trying to make sure that today is not the day that I get pregnancy brain and forget anything!

It is 8a.m. the wedding is at 4:30p.m. and I still need to get my hair and makeup done, pick up the cake, get another pair of shoes as my feet are swollen and the ones I have will not fit and I need to call my brother the chef and make sure that he is going to be on time with the food.

I was so excited for the day it seemed as if I was never going to get Nicole's onesie fastened. Mika sat on the edge of his bed and talked my ear off as usual but today I did not mind all of the repeat questions, like mommy whose house are we going to. After answering this question maybe twenty times we were finally on our way out the door and headed to the car.

When I reached their grandmothers home Ms. Veronica who is actually my soon to be husbands grandmother but the kids call her grandma too. As for me I call her Ms. V. She is a strong woman and the back bone of her family. I am so blessed to be marring such a great guy but I am even more blessed to have such a great woman in my life! She has taught me a lot and I am looking forward to having her in mine and the children's life.

After getting the kids out of the car as always I did not have to ring the doorbell. Ms. V just always seems to know when I pull up in the yard. I saw the screen door open and I hear her soft voice saying come on sugaboogers, your mommy has to go run some errands.

I placed baby girl in her arms and heard Mika walking into the kitchen. The kitchen is where we all went when we entered Ms. V's house. There was always something good waiting for us! Usually some freshly made banana bread which we all looked forwarded to.

I said Ms. V are you ready for today? She smiled and said I am happy for this day I love ya girl. I turned my head to look back over my shoulder at her as I walked quickly to the car saying, I love you too sugabooger she laughed and said girl you crazy.

I hit the freeway doing about 80 miles per hour weaving in and out of traffic. That is my normal speed I keep promising myself I am going to slow down. I was praying I did not get stopped by the police. I wasn't so much worried about the fine as I was the time I would lose waiting for my license to be ran and for the ticket to be written. You can definitely tell that I was 20 years old.

I know go ahead and say it. Yes, I am 20 years old and I am about to be a mother 3 children. So what! I am about to be a married 20 year old with three children.

I pull up to the hair salon with about 10 minutes to spare before my appointment.

The salon was run by my sister Tee when I walk in everyone is full of smiles and excited for me. My sister says today is the day are you ready. My smile was so big that I could hardly answer. I finally replied yes I am ready. Everyone in my family absolutely adored my fiancé Lamar. He fit into my family my mother loved, my sisters that he was help full and my brothers that he was a good man. What my family thought was important to me because I was the baby of the family I was spoiled by all of my family and because Lamar spoiled me everyone thought he was great.

I first saw Lamar when I was hanging out over my girlfriends Sheila's house. It was a hot Saturday afternoon when one of our other friends Michelle called to see what we were doing. We let her know we were just hanging out eating and watching movies. She said that she was going to have this guy drop her off so that she could hang out with us. Only a few hours had gone by when a blue car pulled up and Michelle got out. Sheila and I were being nosey and wanted to see what guy dropped her off so we went outside on the front porch before the car pulled off. It was a light skin, brown eyed guy. When Michelle got in the house we asked 50 questions and she simply let us know this was a guy that worked at a sandwich shop and wanted to take her out on a date but she was not really interested. At that time he was just a guy that possibly was seeing or interested in our friend Michelle.

My mother was sick so myself and my 2 year old son moved into the home of my friend Tabitha and her mother Sherrel. Due to my mothers illness I did not want my son crying and bothering her I wanted her to be able to rest and not worry about us. This was a choice I made on my own my mother did not agree with my decision but I knew it was the best thing for her. Tabitha started dating a guy by the name of Craig. Craig did not have a car so he would catch rides over to see Tabitha with his friends. Once night when Craig walked in the door I was watching television and noticed a tall guy walking in behind him. I looked and I thought I have seen this guy someplace before but due to this not being my company I quickly left the living room. Tabitha called me in the room and said Craig's cousin wanted to know your name. I asked her why she said because he thinks your cute. I asked her does he know I have a baby. She said yes and I said I thought so. She asked me what I meant by that. I explained that it appears that most guys think that you are easy after you have a child and I am sure he does want to talk to me. She said Chantel I think that Lamar is a really nice guy and he asked his cousin about you so maybe he has good intentions. She rolled her eyes at me and said you don't want to be by yourself with that baby forever do you. I rolled my eyes back even though I don't think she way it because she was walking out of the room but I said if it protects my heart I am fine with being single. I thought about her she was just crying over Craig because he did not call her for two days and now she is all in love because he came over again. If it has to be like that then I'm good!

After Lamar dropped off his cousin several times we started talking and Tabitha was right he was a really nice guy. and he took a great interest in me and my son. All of the attention was welcomed! I noticed that Craig stopped coming over with Lamar as much and then finally he did not come over anymore. I noticed that Lamar coming over without Craig started to weigh on the relationship that Tabitha and I had.

We had started to argue over small things to her saying one day you think your all that because Lamar buys you jewelry and takes you out. Jealously had reared its ugly head. I knew then that our sisterly relationship was over and it was time for my son and I to move out.

I spoke to Lamar about what was going on in the house between Tabitha and myself and to my surprise. He found a place for us to live that I could call home and not have to be in limbo with living arrangements. I was shocked but over joyed that he really wanted to be with me and my son. After being together a little over a year I found out I was pregnant with our baby girl. When she was born I felt like my life was perfect. At that point I did not want any additional children I had my family.

As you see the joke was on me because here I go again I am pregnant but I am not unhappy about being pregnant because I am on my way to changing my last name and when this baby comes I will have the same last name as he does.

Now that you know how we made it to this day our wedding day. Let me tell this girl to lift me finger waves a little higher so that they look good in my head piece. It's amazing how when you look away the hair dresser starts doing what they want to your head. I don't know what she is thinking about today is my wedding day and everything has to be perfect.

Once my hair is the way I want it now it is time to get my make-up done for some reason I am the hold up now. I just burst into tears for no apparent reason I don't know if I am crying because of my harmones or because of my nerves. Nothing in Lamar and our relationship has been conventional and today is no exception. Since I could not stop crying I picked up the phone and called Lamar. He said he was just getting out of the chair at the barber shop and he was on his way. Of course all of the ladies at the barber shop was saying no you can't see him. I was like why not I sleep in the same bed he did last night and I can see my man if I want to.

I heard the music when he pulled up at the salon. I instantly jumped up out of the chair and met him at the front door. I was in tear and he was looking pissed. I said what's wrong he said nothing who is messing with you. I sucked up all those tears and I felt all warm inside. He was pissed because he thought they did something to me. That's my man ya'll! He was going to mess you heifers up about his baby.

When I got myself back together I realized the time and ran back to get my make-up done. My sister had already left to go get dressed so I did not have anyone to assure me that my make-up was correct. I have never been a make-up girl. My natural beauty was enough for me so I was not sure if I looked okay. I was about to cry again but I really did not have time to keep breaking down. I dashed out the door to pick up the cake.

After getting the cake, my sister called to let me know she when and found me a satin pair of slippers. I was so glad because I was pressed for time. I still need to go pick up the kids. As I hit the freeway going to get the kids my phone rang. It was Lamar he let me know that he had picked up the kids and gotten them dress. I was so grateful that all I had to do was go home and get dressed. In my mind all I could think was having a partner is great! Again I was smiling ear to ear trying to figure out how did I get so blessed? Everyone was telling us you can see each other but I did not get why. He had already seen my wedding dress. He is my best friend I did not do anything without him. I wanted him to see me in my wedding dress with my hair and make-up it anything was out of place I trusted him to help me fix it.

When I arrived the kids were studding in their wedding attire Nicole sitting in her high chair and Mika on the couch so that neither one of them gets anything on their clothes. I smiled thinking to myself girl you have some beautiful babies.

When I opened the door to the room, I almost messed up my make-up as tears welled up in my eyes from the appears of my future husband. I saw this tall, light skin, light brown eyed brother standing there nervously putting on his suit jacket. He was perfect to me and he was about to be my husband. That smile took over again. I was thinking man I can't wait to get your fine ass out of that suit. After coming out of the trance I ran to the restroom to take my show and get myself dressed.

In true Lamar fashion he opened the restroom door ever so slowly and said you look beautiful you don't need make-up but damn you look good! That was all I needed to hear, that he thought I looked good.

After getting out of the shower I was trying to lotion my swollen feet. Again the door opened and it this white suit Lamar was ready to kneel and lotion my feet. I screamed no I got it. He laughed and said women you don't have to do anything by yourself ever again and he put lotion over my entire body. Jokingly I said boy go on now this is why I am pregnant now.

After I got myself ready Lamar stood in the small hallway smiling I did not need for him to say a word as I knew I looked good and his smile just confirmed it. His smile went away when the alarm clock went off and he yelled we have go we are going to be late to our own wedding. We both grabbed a child and out the door we went.

When we pulled up all of our guest were already at the church all but my friend LaLa. LaLa and I had been friends for years and not seeing her car made me feel a little uneasy. I mentioned to Lamar that I did not see her car and he said all the people we need are here. I instantly calmed down he had that effect on me he always knew what to do or say when I felt uneasy.

With LaLa out of my mind we stepped out of the car and it started raining. I was thinking why is it raining on my wedding day is this meant to be? When Lamar took off his jacket and covered my head I knew this would be okay but when I say him run back to the car and get each child one at a time and wrap them in his jacket and bring them to me I knew that we were in good hands and I was ready to get married.

After getting married we danced the night away with family and friends. As we danced I whispered in Lamar's ear do you think LaLa is okay I can't believe that she missed our wedding. He whispered back today is our day it did not matter if it was just us. I understood what he meant but I did not understand what would make my good friend miss my wedding.

Once the wedding came to an end and the kids had gone with family members we headed for out night together. We did not have a lot of money at all by Ms. V gave us a hotel say for our wedding gift. Once we got to the hotel we were both thinking that this is going to be the best sexual experience of our life. However, we are parents to a 6 month old and a 3 year old and we had been running all day. Once we laid down it was lights out. However, at about 4 am I was awakened to soft kissed on my neck and his large hands caressing my butt from that point I was definitely awake. After, our sessions were over we fell asleep in each other's arms until about 10 am at this time we gathered our things to go pick up the kids and start our life as Mrs. and Mr. Pickens.

At the time I was working at a fast food restaurant and Lamar was working at a factory so money was very tight. We are now approaching out 3 year anniversary and things have changed. We now have three children I have just given birth to a baby boy also named Lamar and his father and I are growing apart. I feel like motherhood is taking a toll on me. Lately I have been feeling like maybe I am going through postpartum depression. Lamar is trying to make me feel beautiful and be a loving husband but I am feeling like I just want out.

One afternoon while taking the children to the park to burn off some energy. I noticed a guy that was there with this son he was staring at me. It was flattering to see someone other than Lamar thought I was beautiful. He walked over and asked me for my phone number I quickly game him my number. As soon as I did I felt horrible. I told him no you can call me I am married. He laughed and said are you sure your married because you lit up when I asked you for your number like a single woman.

On my drive home those words played in my head and I felt horrible. I knew I loved my husband and I could not explain why I was feeling trapped or like I wanted out but what I did know is that I loved my family.

It seemed as if Lamar and I was doing nothing but arguing and the point had come for something to change so he decided that he would go stay at Ms. V's house and we could try dating each other again until we figured out what was going wrong in our marriage. During this time Lamar started to take interest in someone at his job and I only knew because Ms. V did not approve and told me what was happening with Lamar and the Co-worker. I never really spoke to Lamar about it but one night he came back to the apartment that we shared together and said baby we need to move from this place so that our family survives. I did not ask any questions I just said okay because I knew I loved my family more than anything.

He reached out to his family in North Carolina and off we went. We left Maryland and everything behind but our family. When we first arrived in Maryland life was very hard. The girl that Lamar us to take to from his old place of employment was calling. That let me know that he feeling for her greater than what I thought. He had given her the phone number to his cousins house.

I did not say anything I just hoped that it would go away. I felt the distance that had come in our marriage and I was scared. I was scared that I was losing my best friend and my love.

We both keep working really hard and saving our money it took us three months to save enough money to get our own apartment but I was hopeful. I was hopeful that by being in our own space again we could get back to loving each other. I understood that we were young and that things happen I just wanted us to be okay.

Once we moved into our own apartment it seemed as if things got back on track. We started talking again and hang out with each other and it did not seem forced it was just us being us. It felt so good to be back in this place.

One evening when we were laying on the couch watching television after we put the kids to bed. Lamar apologized to me and said he would never do anything to hurt me again. That made my heart smile.

However, I do feel like the devil used me. I because the weak link in our marriage, for years everything was perfect.

Of course nothing is perfect and I started to see life in a whole new light. I was no longer that young girl with a baby that needed saving but I was now a women that could take care of herself. I once again started to feel restless and once I was honest with myself I never really trusted Lamar after knowing he was doing whatever with his co-worker. So I was always wondering was my great husband really great or was I just being fooled. This was something we never spoke about it was just something that I always tried to keep in the back of my mind but lately it is coming more and more to the forefront of my mind.

One day while I was at work I had a guard come up to me and say I have been watching you. In my mind I was like this is the worst line I have ever heard. However, said I have not been watching you and walked off. The next day when I came to work there were 3 dozen long stem roses at my desk and the card said I noticed your ring on your hand so I am sure you're not available but I just wanted to give a rose some roses. Signed the guard that you don't see.

This peaked my interest why did he send me flowers what did he see in me to make him say anything to me. He knew I was married so what made him do this. So me being curious I went to the guard desk and asked. Why did you give me roses if you know I am married? I am sure you have seen me with my husband he comes to eat lunch with me from time to time. Do you not respect marriages? He replied what question would you like me to answer first. I thought to myself smart ass. I replied which ever one you would like to answer. He said yes I respect marriage I have been married twice. Yes I have seen you with your husband but I have not seen you smile so I thought I would give you flowers. It's not often that I am at a loss for words but I was at a loss for words so I just walked off.

When I got to work the next day I had a 3 foot bear at my desk. With the same signature from the guard that you don't see. This time I did not walk out to the desk and say anything. I just picked up my desk phone and called Lamar. I wanted to hear his voice because I was feeling a little weak at this moment. Hearing his voice made me go to the desk and tell the guard. Do not send me another gift I am a happily married woman. The guard smiled at me and said I am Shad but you can call me whatever you like over dinner. I could not believe the nerve of this man. However, his confidence was cute.

When I got home from work Lamar was already gone he worked the night shift at the hospital. After getting the kids feed and in the bed. I pulled out my work laptop and looked up employee log and I found Shad. I called his work number not knowing that he had a work phone that he took home daily. When he answered he said thank you for calling Chantel. Once he said my name I could not hang up like I wanted to. I said how did you know it was me he said caller ID ma'am. I laughed nervously and we talked about life for hours. I felt as if I had known him forever. Talking to him after putting the kids to bed because a nightly thing. I did not feel like I was doing anything wrong because I did not talk to him at work nor had I gone out with him. To me it was simply passing the time at night while Lamar was at work.

One night Shad asked me to meet him for a drink I told him I didn't drink but was up for food. At this time the kids were out of town spending time with my mother for the summer, Lamar was at work and I was bored. That is how I justified going to dinner with Shad. Since Shad and I had been talking on the phone now for over 6 months eating dinner with him was just like eating dinner with a friend. I had no idea that I was going to like spending time with him as much as I did.

The next day Lamar and I went out on our weekly date night but all I could do was think about Shad. I knew then I was in trouble.

After Lamar asking me over dinner several times where was I? He could tell that I was not present. When I looked up into his big brown eyes I had to come clean I told him that I had been spending my nights while he was at working talking to this person named Shad. You could see the tears form in his eyes and then the anger on this face. I instantly started saying how sorry I was he did not want to hear anything I had to say. We left the restaurant and the drive home was uncomfortably silent.

The silence went on for days and then weeks. Until one day Lamar walked into the living room and said I am leaving. I am going back to Maryland. We both cried but thought maybe we will get through this. However, after he had gone I started spending more time with Shad and it had turned romantic. Once day I received an email from Lamar saying that he found his true love and I lost it. I think that I was hurt to know that we were truly over. I do believe in my mind that we were just going through something even though I had totally crossed the line by laying with another man.

One morning I logged into my computer and noticed that I had an email from Lamar. This was strange because he had my phone number we stilled spoke on the phone. So before I clicked to read the email I felt early strange and nervous. I felt like this email was about to change my life forever. Even though we were separated I always had hopes of me finding my way back to him and us making our family whole again. I think I always thought that we can have bumps we are a young family just trying to get it right.

The email started off my saying I found the person I love. I did not or could not ready anymore. I was a very lengthy email but all I could read was that one line. I sat at the computer sobbing uncontrollably.

I was hurt and then I because angry thinking you did it to me and I let it go. What a selfish thing to think I know. I just wanted things to go back the way they were. I was so angry because I honestly could not tell you why we got here. Why were we in a place where we could not find each other? I started thinking was our love ever real? Was I ready to be married? Did I know what love way? Did I know how to love? Did I know how to be loved? Why did I always have a feeling that our love was not as strong as I wanted to think it was? Simply WHY?

I became blind with rage and I wanted him to tell me in my face that he had found his love. I had never made him answer for anything I felt that he had done wrong but this time I wanted an answer and I was going to get it. Not via email but face to face!

I called Mika down stairs and asked him to pack clothes for he and his siblings because we were going to Maryland for a few days.

In the mist of me getting myself somewhat together my phone rang. I said hello without looking at the caller ID. One the other end of the phone it was Shad. He was not the voice I wanted to hear but I snappy with him. I let him know that I had received this email and I was going to Maryland for a few days.

He was silent for a moment before asking me why? I asked him what he meant by why. I was married and my husband is saying he found his love and it is not me. He quickly knocked me down a peg and said didn't you find your love? Am I not your love because you are mine?

At that very moment I understood the full magnitude to what I had allowed to happen. Not only have I stepped out of my marriage but I have another man that really loves me. Now I have hurt two people. Yes my husband did things to hurt me but I am not this person I am better than what my behavior has indicated I am.

All I could say is can I call you back. He yelled on the other end of the phone "NO" you can't call me back talk to me now please. This man had never raised his voice at me he had never been anything but kind.

He said baby please talk to me, I am in this too and I love you and the kids. Please tell me what are you going to do are you going to fix your marriage or are you going to end it so that we can be a family?

I was trying to listen to him but honestly all he was doing was pissing me off. I said somewhat snappy my marriage means more to me than any fling or anyone. As soon as the words left my lips I felt bad. I did not want to hurt him he did not deserve it but I wanted him to understand no matter what is going on right now I do have real love for my family. I realized then that I made a huge mistake that may cost me everything.

Shad once again became quite. I did not give him a chance to say anything else I hung up the phone. I ran up the stairs to make sure the kids had some clothes in the suitcase and then I grab somethings out of my closet and we all headed out to the car.

When I got to Maryland I had the landlord open the apartment that Lamar had rented.

So much was going on in my mind that I did not realize today was Valenties day but I was about to remember.

When I walked into Lamars apartment I saw rose petals on the floor and when I walked into the bedroom no one was there. However there was a photo on the dresser and it was a photo of Lamar and LaLa. Instantly I was outraged and started destroying the house. Once I had destroyed all things that I could I realized my children were crying. I instantly felt horrible and I started crying. I apologized to them for my actions.

The only person I knew to call that would give me sound advise was Ms. V. I called her and let her know what I found in the apartment and that Lamar was sleeping with my friend. Sayhing these words to her out of my mouth brought on another flood of emotions. In that instance it made me understand why she had not come to my wedding and it made me understand why I always felt so uneasy in my marriage.

Ms. V said I am getting in my car now and I am on my way to you. She asked me to please not try and drive with the children I was too emotional. I told her that I would stay put until she got there and that is what I did.

I was so angry that when I called Lamar's phone I am sure he did not even understand what I was saying but rest assure he did understand that I was in his apartment.

He pulled up in the car before Ms. V made it but when he pulled up he had the nerve to have LaLa in the car with him. I was so angry that it felt like I went blink for a moment everything went black.

The funny thing is that LaLa said "Happy Valentine's" to me Chantel my thought was bitch do you not know I will kill you? Lamar told her to get in his car and leave. She drove off and all I could think is did you just tell that bitch to leave in our car.

So many things were going through my head but the major thing was how long had this been going one has this motherfucker really been playing me from day one was all of this really a joke. I went from feeling bad for my actions with Shad to feeling justified.

I really can not remember what Lamar said to me it all sounded like bullshit so I was not even listening. In my mind all I could think was this motherfucker. This motherfucker has been playing me from day one and this bitch that I have helped played me too.

All I can remember is the police were called luckily no one went to jail this time and LaLa pulling back up and Lamar getting in the car and leaving.

Ms. V told me and the kids to come stay at her house but because I was so discombobulated I did not want to be around anyone. The kids and I actually stayed in Lamar's apartment because I wanted to take it all in. I wanted to feel the hurt.

The next morning I went to talk to Ms. V and she was so upset at both of us and the way we handled our marriage. One thing about her she was fair so she was not letting me get off easy either!

She said do you love Lamar I said yes but was it all fake has he been messing with her for years. Is that why he wanted me to stay away from her? Of course she did not have the answers.

She told me all she could say is if the love is true and mean really true there is not a person alive that can take away. She said baby I can't tell if the love you all have is true only the two of you know this.

I took those words to heart. I put the kids back in the car and we took the drive back to North Carolina. On the way there I keep thinking the way you meet him is the same way you lost him. He dropped off someone that was your friend and now he is laying with someone you were a friend to. However, if the love is true it will fix itself. I wiped the tears away from my face turned up the music and started weaving in and out of traffic with a smile on my face. Only God knows my next Valentine's Day will go.

Made in the USA
Columbia, SC
25 August 2022